AM FAMOUS

Tara Luebbe and Becky Cattie

illustrated by Joanne Lew-Vriethoff

Albert Whitman & Company
Chicago, Illinois

To Derick W. and Becky S.—my literary glam squad—TL
For Hannah, my favorite diva—BC
To Maarten with love—JLV

Library of Congress Cataloging-in-Publication data is on file with the publisher.

Text copyright © 2018 by Tara Luebbe and Becky Cattie
Illustrations copyright © 2018 by Joanne Lew-Vriethoff
Hardcover edition first published in the United States of America in 2018 by Albert Whitman & Company
Paperback edition first published in the United States of America in 2021 by Albert Whitman & Company
ISBN 978-0-8075-3453-3 (paperback)
ISBN 978-0-8075-3445-8 (ebook)

Printed in China
10 9 8 7 6 5 4 3 2 1 RRD 24 23 22 21 20
Design by Jordan Kost

For more information about Albert Whitman & Company,
visit our website at www.albertwhitman.com.

am famous.

I am an actress,

a singer,

and a dancer.

Daddy says I'm also a diva...
whatever that is.

A Star Is Born

I've been famous for as long as I can remember.

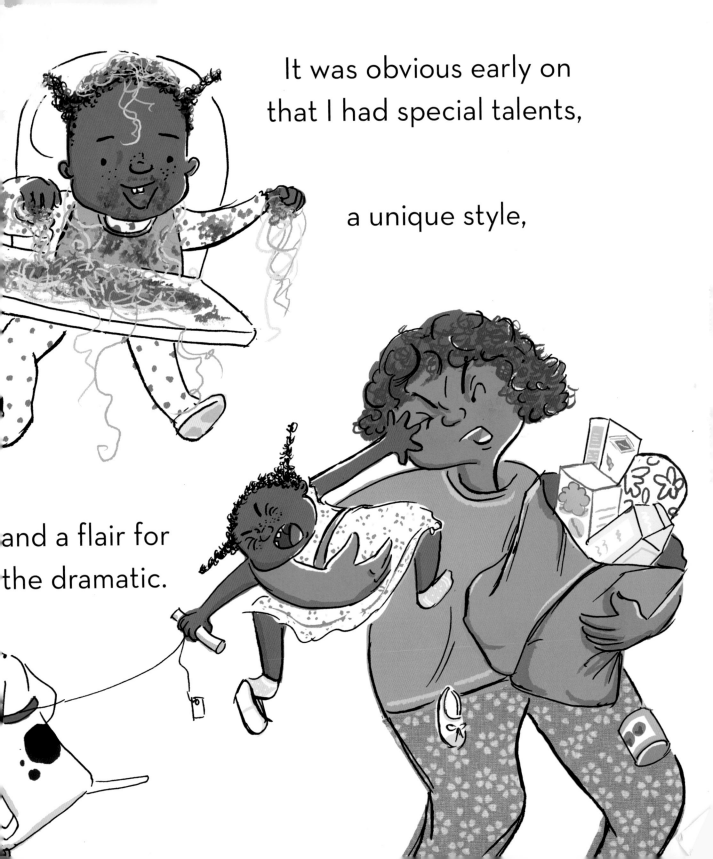

It was obvious early on
that I had special talents,

a unique style,

and a flair for
the dramatic.

Because I am famous,
I get special treatment
wherever I go.

I have my own chef, driver, and housekeeper.

My fan club spoils me.

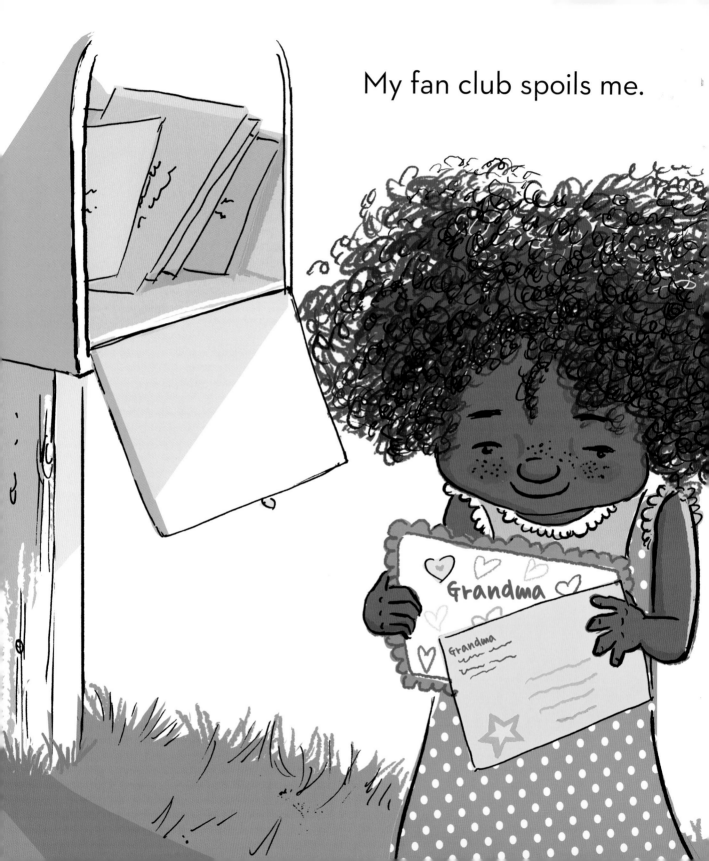

i my movies go viral.

KielysMommy

436 views • 18 likes

46

The paparazzi follow me everywhere. In showb
that means photographers who take pictures of
famous people, like me.

Sometimes it's annoying.

They bother me when I'm dining.

They chase me while I'm ariv

They invade my privacy!
"Do something cute," they beg.
Oh, the price of fame!

Tonight I'm performing at Grandpa's birthday pa
This will be my biggest show yet.

My stylist arrives.
We discuss the right look.

I hit the red carpet.

Wait! I need my sunglasses.
Famous people *always*
wear sunglasses.
  "Break a leg!" Daddy says.
In showbiz, that means
good luck.

It's a packed house.

I've never seen so many fans.

Showtime!

For act one
I sing Grand
favorite song

Uh-oh! What were
the words again?
Just keep smiling.
The show must go on!
La la la...

Intermission.

Now for act two...

I dazzle them with my latest dance moves.

Ouch! Just keep smiling.

The show *must* go on!

And the grand finale...

How humiliating! I'll never work in this town again.

What's happening? Is that applause?
It's my fans!

They still love me, no matter what.
And that's the *best* part about being a star.

I am still famous.

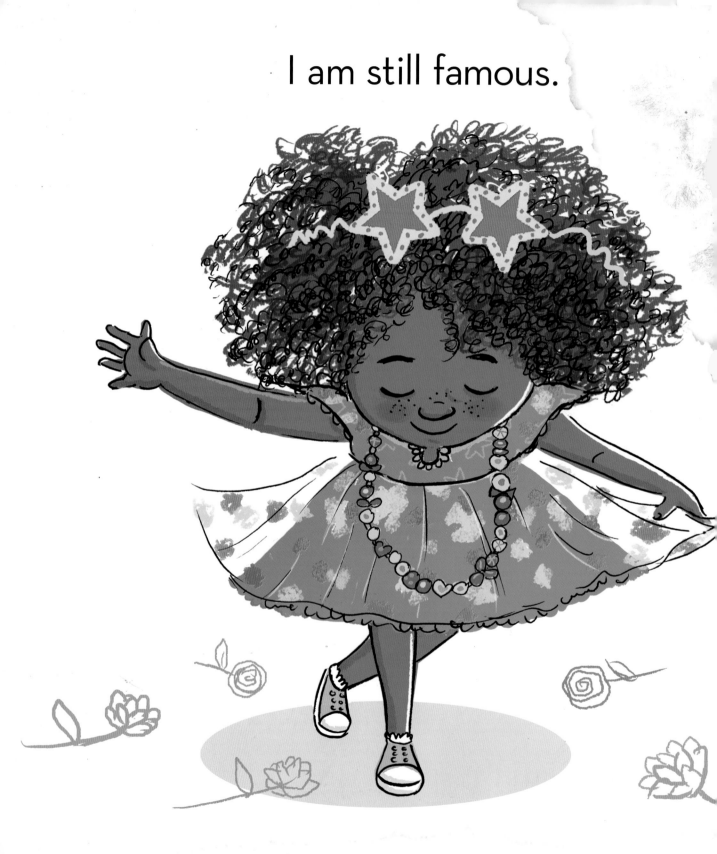